The Story of the Snow Children

First published in German in 1905 under the title *Was Marilenchen erlebte?*
English version © Floris Books, Edinburgh 2005
This mini edition 2012. Second printing 2014
All rights reserved. No part of this publication may be
reproduced without prior permission of
Floris Books, 15 Harrison Gardens, Edinburgh
www.florisbooks.co.uk
British Library CIP Data available
ISBN 978-086315-909-1
Printed in Malaysia

The Story of
the Snow Children

Sibylle von Olfers

Floris Books

Poppy looked out of the window. She was all alone in the house, for her mother had just stepped out but seemed to be gone an awfully long time.

Outside all was still, and the sky was grey. But what was that? Suddenly Poppy saw lots of snowflakes dancing and jumping as they fell.

"Come out and play with us, Poppy. We'll take you to the Snow Queen."

There were hundreds and hundreds of snow children, beautiful and white, swirling and twirling, calling out to her.

Poppy dressed up warmly in her coat, hat and thick gloves. She ran into the garden to watch the wild game.

Laughing and giggling, the snow children called out for Swirly-Wind to come with her silvery sledge.

Poppy sat on the sledge – and away she was pulled, over hedges and woods, with the snow children dancing around.

They came to a castle of ice all shining white – the turrets like sugar, the walls smooth as glass.

There Poppy stood in awe before the Snow Queen's throne.

The Queen, with the royal Princess on her lap, welcomed Poppy to the grand festival.

For today was the Princess's birthday. A huge feast was spread out for the guests. There was snowy white chocolate and sweet ice-cold tea.

Snowmen (who usually just stand still and quiet) hurried about serving the delicious food. When they were done they stood to attention around the white walls.

Then the Princess took Poppy for a stroll around her garden. A thousand different kinds of wonderful flowers sparkled like crystal glass. The ground was polished like a mirror, and the leaves, plants and grass were all snowy white.

Suddenly a trumpet fanfare announced the dance. A hundred lanterns had been lit in the great ice hall.

The snow children's lively dancing led them all around the Snow Queen's throne – whirling faster and faster until Poppy felt as if her feet would drop off.

Poppy sank down in the snow. Her ears and eyes had had enough and her body ached. Now all she wanted was to go home.

The Princess cried, "Oh, stay with me – we'll play exciting games. And I'll give you the biggest icicles and lots of snowballs."

But the Snow Queen said wisely, "Quick, fetch the sleigh. Don't worry, Poppy, my snowman will drive you home."

In no time at all the sleigh stood by the gate with four strong snow bears harnessed in front. Poppy said a fond farewell to everyone.

The sleigh stopped at last before Poppy's house. Her mother stood at the door and welcomed her. "You're back at last."

And Poppy told her mother about all her adventures and the wonderful things that had happened.

Perhaps, one day, you too can ride on a silver sledge to the Snow Kingdom.

Sibylle von Olfers

Sibylle von Olfers' (1881–1916) blend of natural observation and simple design has led to comparisons with Kate Greenaway and Elsa Beskow.

She was born the third of five children in a castle in East Prussia. Encouraged by her aunt, she trained at art college. Her beauty attracted many admirers and suitors, but she remained aloof and distant from the "useless world of the aristocrats".

At the age of twenty-five she joined the Sisters of Saint Elizabeth, an order of nuns. As well as teaching art in the local school, she wrote and illustrated a number of children's books. Tragically, she died at the age of thirty-four from a lung infection.

The Story of the Snow Children is her first book, published in 1905. Her other books include *The Story of the Root Children* (1906), *The Story of the Rabbit Children* (1906), *The Story of Little Billy Bluesocks* (1906), *Princess in the Forest* (1909), *The Story of the Wind Children* (1910), *The Story of the Butterfly Children* (1916) and *The Story of King Lion* (1923).